SHADES OF LIFE

STORY OF DIFFERENT PHASES IN LIFE

AF558867

SANSKRITI KAUL

Copyright © Sanskriti Kaul
All Rights Reserved.

This book has been self-published with all reasonable efforts taken to make the material error-free by the author. No part of this book shall be used, reproduced in any manner whatsoever without written permission from the author, except in the case of brief quotations embodied in critical articles and reviews.

The Author of this book is solely responsible and liable for its content including but not limited to the views, representations, descriptions, statements, information, opinions and references ["Content"]. The Content of this book shall not constitute or be construed or deemed to reflect the opinion or expression of the Publisher or Editor. Neither the Publisher nor Editor endorse or approve the Content of this book or guarantee the reliability, accuracy or completeness of the Content published herein and do not make any representations or warranties of any kind, express or implied, including but not limited to the implied warranties of merchantability, fitness for a particular purpose. The Publisher and Editor shall not be liable whatsoever for any errors, omissions, whether such errors or omissions result from negligence, accident, or any other cause or claims for loss or damages of any kind, including without limitation, indirect or consequential loss or damage arising out of use, inability to use, or about the reliability, accuracy or sufficiency of the information contained in this book.

Made with ♥ on the Notion Press Platform
www.notionpress.com

The book is dedicated to my mother, father, and grandparents...... I am always grateful to them for supporting me always.

Contents

Foreword

This book is the first edition of the series. This book shows the journey of a girl and her parents. This story talks about how a girl named Kizie cope up with different situations in her life and how she learned to face every situation and grow in her life. This story shows, how small and big incidents can change one's life completely. One can see how a decision took by Kaira's parents can affect her and how she is affected. It is a short story, and it is divided into parts.

Preface

This a story close to my heart, as I wanted to write this story since I was in grade 8th. Initially, this story was a short story but then I divided this story into parts describing different stages of Kizie's life. I never thought I would start writing or would actually be able to turn my story in form of a book but I did and that was the best deicison.

Acknowledgements

I would like to thank my mother who has always been my support system. Who actually supported me in every step of my life including supporting me in writing this book. Apart from my mother I would like to thank my frinds, as they have been my support throughout my journey other than my mother and who have always motivated me to continue writing whenever I felt low or wanted to quit writing this book.

Prologue

This book is the continution of Different Shades of Life. The previous book talked about thw lifce of Kizie and the emotional turmoil she faced through her teenage life and how she actually dealed with the problems and situations that came into her way.

Kizie was Kaira's and Vihaaan's only daughter. She was the most pampered kid in her family. Mamta and Sanjay had a love marriage which was not approved by Kaira's family but eventually everyone had to accept Mamta's decision because she was being all stubborn with her decision.

After one year of Kaira's and Vihaan's marriage, Kizie was born, who was pampered by almost everyone in the family but it was not always happiness in Kizie's life. After a certain time, things turned ugly for everyone when Kizie and Vihaan got divorced. That was something which affected Kizie the most and that is when incidents started to happen in Kizie's life. As Kizie's grandmother expired and then with six months her father also expired. Now this was the time where Kizie had to understand her emotions and balance her social, emotional, and academic life.

This book is the continution of Different Shades of Life. The previous book talked about thw lifce of Kizie and the emotional turmoil she faced through her teenage life and how she actually dealed with the problems and situations that came into her way.

Kizie was Kaira's and Vihaan's only daughter. She was the most pampered kid in her family. Kaira and Vihaan had a love marriage which was not approved by Kaira's family but eventually everyone had to accept Kaira's decision because she was being all stubborn with her decision.

After one year of Kaira's and Vihaan's marriage, Kizie was born, who was pampered by almost everyone in the family but it was not always happiness in Kizie's life. After a certain time, things turned ugly for everyone when Kaira and Vihaan got divorced. That was something which affected Kizie the most and that is when incidents started to happen in Kizie's life. As her grandmother expired and then with six months her father also expired. Now this was the time where Kizie had to understand her emotions and balance her social, emotional, and academic life.

Shades of Life goes on to discuss Kizie's experience after losing her father and how she coped with her feelings.

"It is Kaira's responsibility to look after her father as she didn't have a family unlike her other sisters."

"Sometimes you just have to concentrate on small happiness rather than waiting for big happiness in your family."

"Kizie learned to balance her emotions, social life, and academics."

"Kizie scored really good marks in her 12th grade."

"It is mamta's responsibility to look after her father as she didn't have a family unlike her other sisters."

"Sometimes you just have to concentrate on small happiness rather than waiting for big happiness in your family."

"Kizie learned to balance her emotions, social life, and academics."

"Kizie scored really good marks in her 12th grade."

Character Sketch

Kizie (Main lead): - A fun-loving, chirpy, joyful, and happy child. But with time she changed. She didn't change, time changed her. You'll get to know more about her in upcoming chapters. She loved her parents and grandparents a lot. And she was always emotionally attached to her grandmother more than her own mother.

Vihaan (Kizie's Dad): - Kizie's superhero, best friend, and world's best dad for her. Joyful and cheerful. Treats her daughter like a princess. Kizie was a complpete daddy's princess. Her demand have always been a command for him. Though Vihaan always treated Kizie as a princess but he also made sure that he makes Kizie bold enough to face the world on her own even when he is not there for her.

Kaira (Kizie's mother and 2nd daughter of Bhavna and Tarsem): - A superwoman for her daughter. Strict towards her daughter when comes to her studies and handles everything. She is a superwoman for Kizie. Though she was strict with Kizie when it comes to studies but over the time their relation changed. And like, Vihaan even she made sure that she teaches everything to Kizie and make her bold enough.

Bhavna (Kizie's maternal grandmother): - A mother-like figure for Kizie. Kizie used to call her Nani. She is a very calm and composed person, understanding, manages everything, and cares for everyone. She never used to say a word or speak in a loud voice.

Tarsem (Kizie's maternal grandfather): - A very real and good grandfather and dad. Always supported Kizie. He used to pamper Kizie a lot and fulfill her wishes like a magician.

Anika (Kizie's masi and 1st daughter of Bhavna and Tarsem): - A homemaker and more of family and traditional type for whom nothing mattered apart from what her husband said to her.

Disha (Kizie's masi and 3rd daughter of Bhavna and Tarsem): - A teacher like a figure to Kizie for her as she has spent a good amount of time with her. But as the story progress the relationship between Kizie and Disha changed. And same like Anika, even Disha priortised her husband and family over anything else.

Sana (Kizie's masi and 4th daughter of Bhavna and Tarsem): - She lives in Australia with her husband and two kids. Initially didn't share a good bond with her but with time they started sharing a different and good bond with her. But gradually again there were rift between Kizie because of the things Sana said.

Ayush: - Kizie's mama and Bhavna and Tarsem's son.

Uttkarsh- Disha's son and the first boy in the family. As he is youngest one, he was always pampered by everyone. Specially by Kizie as a aby was born in the family after a long time and Kizie just wanted to keep Uttkarsh with her all the time. Both of them shared a typical sibling type of a relationship.

1

Chapter One

How would you personally define life? A life is a mixture of love, happiness, ups, downs, and sadness. Naming four or five emotions can't describe life right? Maybe this is the only reason why the previous book was titled as the "Different Shades of Life." Maybe because it described Kizie's life perfectly with all the emotions that she has gone through. Can life be totally smooth? It is smooth but with adventures in them. Though we might see other people's life being smooth, but sometimes that's not the truth, we might not see the reality from far.

Kizie wasn't in a good mental state after loosing her grandmother and father in just six months. It isn't easy for anyone. Being in 10th grade, where students think about their grades and thinking on which stream they will be choosing in respect to their career even Kizie would be thinking the same but alas! she was lost. Lost thinking what she exactly want to do. Lost in another world thinking how the life would be without her grandmother and father being around her. Who would be there to listen her blabber, handle her childishness, pamper her and love her like anything. Though Kizie did have her grandfather and mother but every person holds a certain place in everyone's life and no one can replace it. No matter how many people Kizie had around her, no one could fill the gaps for what she shared with her grandmother and father. Everyone has their own place in one's life and it can't be filled by anyone. Losing yourself for someone can't be the option that you would opt for. You might opt for it irrespective of it being by your side because at the end you have to move on as life doesn't stop for anyone means anyone, no matter what. Coping up and moving forwards is the only option left. Thinking this Kizie tried to move on her life. Though she was trying but still she wasn't able to accept the reality that her dad is no more, she wanted to live in her own world and not accept the reality but till when? Now or later, one has to face the reality. She too did but for a particular time and then again she would get into her own world, not accepting the reality. But who knew what's stored in her life. But then life can not go according to your will, isn't it? Though Kizie wanted to score good marks as she did realise what her ultimate goal was. She might behave in the worst manner but when it comes to her career goals she has always been focused about them but not now, she couldn't focus on them after what all happened in this one year. Where she wanted someone to support her not just to stand with her but she wanted someone to support her emotionally, help her get through this phase of her life. She did have her mum and grandfather with her but how can she expect her mother to support her emotionally when she herself wasn't stable emotionally. Kizie's mother tried to be as strong as possible in front of her but even Kizie knew what exactly her mother was feeling because even she was having similar feelings. Therefore, Kizie had certain expectations from some people but no one kept upto her expectations which just added a fuel to her emotions and irritation towards her extended family. Where she tried to be strong in front of her mother because Kizie didn't want her mother to breakdown seeing her, she herself couldn't be strong when she was alone. With all the turmoil going inside her mind she gave her 10th grade board exams, not knowing how they are going. It was when her result came, she just a gave a sigh of relief thinking that thank god at least she didn't fail her board exams. But for the fact only she was the one who signed in relief but others were stressed about it because with the percentage that Kizie scored she couldn't get admission in the stream in which she wanted, which is commerce. Commerce was not the stream which Kizie wanted to take up but since grade 2, she just had one dream and that was to become a doctor but going with that fact about her marks she knew she can not get PCB and now honestly she didn't even have enough mind to study such tough subjects and score well in them. Therefore, she decided to take up psychology and pursue that as her career, she thought somewhere or the other she will at least get into a career which is related to health. The only difference would be not physical health but mental health. Kizie clearly knew she couldn't study the subjects in humanities stream and she wouldn't score high marks that she could get science stream and somewhere Kizie had a slight idea that she wouldn't be able to do science as now he can't think straight and she hasn't recovered with her loss still. Commerce stream was something which she could do but commerce was also not the stream that Kizie wanted to pursue. If it was as per her choice then she would just study psychology in which she wanted to make her career but that wasn't the option right? And the only reason why commerce was chosen was that Kaira was a tax consultant and she wanted Kizie to study accounts because according to her Kizie didn't have qualities of being a psychologist and as a second career Kaira wanted Kizie to have a back up plan with her studies. After talking and discussing a lot with the teachers she got admission in commerce stream, not only she got an admission but with it she even got one more chance to prove herself. To prove herself that she could do better in her studies and achieve her goals, to become someone she always wanted to and of course to make her parents proud.

If Kizie's life was tragic in 10th grade how do you expect her 11th grade to be? Good? Bad? Horrible? Better or Stable?

Starting of Kizie's 11th grade was a really unstable because if you remember as mentioned in "Different Shades of Life" Kizie lost her mother's grandfather, her grandmother, and her father that too just before her board exams which affected her board exams result badly. But was it easy? She questioned herself, not thinking much she started with her studies without knowing what's stored in future for her. She just thought to go with the flow. With so many things happening after on another one thing which made her happy was her cousin, her masi's (Disha) son. Though Uttkarsh has always been special to Kizie because it was after his birth when Kizie truly felt that she is an elder sister now and he was her baby brother . She already loved him so much but now after so many things happening together Uttkarsh became more special to Kizie. She would tease him, play with him, hug him, and of course love him a lot. Uttkarsh's cute antics would always made Kizie's mood better, though she always loved them but she would also have fights with him. They used to fight with each other on anything and many times Kizie would even scold Uttkarsh a lot but she couldn't stay mad with him for long. Not even for five minutes, as soon as Uttkarsh would get sad Kizie would return to her caring and loving sister forgetting all her anger on him because no matter what she will always love Uttkarsh because he has always been special to her, her baby brother. With all the turmoil in her life, she, her mother, and her grandfather were leading their lives.

As Kizie thought earlier, she was indeed going with the flow and according to her she was giving her best in the studies but alas! Whenever she used to think that she did her best in the tests or exams and she will get good marks, she would end up getting low marks. Kizie wasn't in the good books of teachers, already she didn't score high marks in her 10th grade that she would get commerce stream in her 11th and 12th grade, it was only after talking to teachers and explaining them about the situation Kizie was able to get commerce stream that too without maths and economics, which actually made her happy because she wasn't interested in them at all the only thing Kizie was interested in was psychology. The teachers weren't happy with Kizie at all because firstly she got commerce stream because of the situation she was in and not because of her merit which irritated her teacher specially her accounts teacher and on top of that she wasn't scoring well in her class tests. Somehow, Kizie passed her class tests and now it was time for her mid semester exams. Now, she really had to score well for the exams because if she wouldn't then she again would loose a chance to prove herself. Thinking this, she started to prepare for her mid semester exams. Her exams were going to start in another one and a half month when her grandfather got seriously ill and had to get admitted in hospital. As Kizie wasn't scoring well in her class tests so her teachers asked her not to miss school but when her grandfather was ill and he had to be hospitalised on urgent basis but because of school mum (Kaira) asked her sisters to stay in hospital with Kizie's grandfather so that she can stay with Kizie and she doesn't have to miss her school.

How would you feel when any of your parents get admitted in hospital? Strange right? More than that nervous, anxious, stressed, and so many different emotions you experience in that particular time frame. No matter how many siblings you have each and every child has certain emotions for their parents which no one can compare too, What do you think how would have Kaira's sisters reacted when asked to stay with their father at the hospital? A yes, of course because even they were his daughters and if one can't make it then the others would definitely help them. But this might disappoint you but Kaira's sisters denied. Denied to stay at the hospital but the question here is why? Out of four daughter's Kaira has to be with Kizie because again her school is important and Kaira can not leave Kizie alone at home without anyone being with her. Then it came to Sana, she stays abroad so there is no chance that she would come to India immediately to India. Agreed. But what about the other two, right? What excuses did they give? Anika, being the eldest one, gave the most lame reason. She said that I can't leave my husband and kids for a week and stay at hospital, she did have some feelings but no she can't leave her family for two days and stay in hospital with her father. Ah! Now coming to Ekta. What do you think, what would she have answered? She said yes, she will stay at the hospital. A bit relaxing right? I had hoped, for Kizie's grandfather's sake, that he would be hospitalised with a loved one. I hate to be the bearer of bad news, but she agreed with you and said that I couldn't stay at the hospital without abandoning my husband and son. You can't just leave someone in the hospital, so either you or your friend had to stay. Even if you consider this, do you think you'd actually have the guts to carry it out? This is especially true when dealing with one's own parents. Kizie and Kaira would never even consider something like this. However, in this case, not one of my four daughters has predicted that I will require hospitalisation. Kaira had no choice but to stay at the hospital with her father, so of course Kizie had to come along.

Being hospitalised is neither a vacation nor something that can be easily planned. How long a patient will have to stay in the hospital is always a mystery. Because of this, neither Kaira nor Kizie knew what was going on, but they still went to the hospital to be with Kizie's grandfather rather than leaving him there alone, because no child has the strength of character to leave their parents in the hospital to endure the worst experiences of their lives without them.

Being a doctor is certainly not a simple task; it requires extensive training and hard work over many years. No one said being a doctor would be simple. To be a patient is difficult in and of itself. Who wants to be confined to four walls for who knows how many days with needles, wires, and bland hospital food? Absolutely no one, right? Unfortunately, the patient is the one who must endure this. Although the patient is unable to verbalise the suffering they are experiencing, others are also unable to offer insight into their ordeal. This is because no one can truly appreciate the difficulty of a situation or the steps involved in a process unless they themselves have gone through them. Kizie's grandfather was getting back to normal after three or four days in the hospital, though he still wasn't fully well. After returning home with Kizie and Kaira, he began to feel better; however, as time passed, Kizie noticed that her grandfather wasn't taking his medication as prescribed and was instead discarding them. She was at a loss for what to do, so she confided in her sister Kaira, hoping that she could help her understand why her father was continuing to put his health at risk in spite of knowing the dangers. Mama heard this and had a talk with her dad about it. After an hour of questioning, Kizie's grandfather admitted that, since the passing of Kizie's grandmother, he has lost all motivation to live. Kaira was initially taken aback by this news, but she quickly got over it and tried to convince her father of the importance of his life to her and her sister Kizie. When he showed no signs of changing his mind, however, Kaira decided to break the news to her sisters in private. One the one hand, Kizie's health wasn't great and she was diagnosed with Typhoid, and the doctor asked Kaira to admit Kizie to the hospital, but Kaira knew that she couldn't handle leaving Kizie in the hospital for a week for two reasons: Kizie doesn't like staying in the hospital for even a day, and they can't leave Kizie's grandfather alone in the house with a house help and no one will come to live with him for a week How can they stay in the hospital for a week if they can't even bear to be away from their loved ones for a day? A week ago, Kaira was taking care of her sick father; now she's doing the same for Kizie. Kizie's midterms were coming up, her grandfather's health was declining, and Rashi, Kaira's youngest sister, was planning a two-month visit to India, so she made the decision to treat her at home rather than take her to the hospital. She brought her children to India, and her husband was expected to join them there in two weeks. It was a surprise for Kizie's grandfather when Kaira and she went to pick up Rashi and her children from the airport, and even though he was very weak, he held Rashi's son in his hands with all the love in his eyes for him, and he hugged Rashi's daughter with love. The children have no idea what's going on, but Kaira, Kizie, and rashi know how much he's missed having children around and being able to lavish attention and affection on them. Despite the fact that his health prevented him from doing so, he deeply desired to hold children in his arms. Rashi was scheduled to spend two weeks with Kaira, Kizie, and Kizie's grandfather, but since she is from India, she will also be spending time with his in-laws. She went to meet her in-laws the day after arriving in India. During those two weeks, she and the kids shuttled between her dad's and her in-laws' homes. While Rashi did spend the vast majority of her time with her father, her in-laws visited her and the children frequently. Even though Rashi spent time with her dad, Kaira, and sister, Kizie was still unsatisfied. She didn't understand why her in-laws insisted on frequent visits to their home. Why doesn't she just stay with us and enjoy being with us? Kizie's husband, Mosaji, finally arrived after two weeks, and everyone went to the airport to pick him up, even though he justified his desire to go home immediately. Kizie didn't want to go to the airport, but she knew she had to if she was going to be a part of the group that went to pick him up. That wasn't because she actively disliked him; rather, it was because of events of the past.

Flashback

This Raksha Bandhan was the first time the whole family was together. Rashi, who normally spent her time abroad away from the celebrations, was present this time around. Raksha Bandhan was a big deal for Kizie, and like every year, she got a henna tattoo on her hands to commemorate the occasion. Rashi's daughter was ecstatic after getting henna and was showing her tattoo to her father over video chat, when Kizie arrived and began showing off her own. When Kizie was showing her henna on video call suddenly rashi's daughter said, "you can't show your henna to my father, he is my father not yours." She didn't say anything wrong, she was a child after all and a possessive daughter indeed. Kizie didn't take kindly to this, especially since her father had recently died and she had every right to be possessive about her father as a child, but she also didn't get along with her cousin. Because of what happened, Kizie began to long for her father. Kizie was reminded of how much she missed her own father when she overheard rashi's children chatting with theirs. Since that day, Kizie has avoided any situation in which she would have to observe a father-daughter bond out of fear that she will break down emotionally and physically if she is forced to confront the reality that her father is no longer present. When Kizie was alone with Rashi's children at home, Rashi's daughter said to her, "Your father is no more because he wasn't a good person," and Kizie's mind froze. This was the second incident that made Kizie avoid these situations. Kizie was at a loss for what to do, but she had to take care of the kids, so she waited for Kaira and the others to return before retreating to her room to cry uncontrollably. Rashi entered Kizie's room and saw her in tears; upon seeing Kizie's face, she called Kaira and inquired as to the cause of her sobs. At first Kizie avoided answering her question, but then she realised she couldn't lie to her mother. When Kaira heard the truth, she understood that Kizie had been hurt emotionally as well as physically. Kaira realised this and acted swiftly to treat Kizie and comfort her before her condition deteriorated further. Seeing Kizie's condition, Rashi's daughter realised that she said something bad, and even she got sad seeing

Kizie, but the damage was done. Though this hurt Kizie, she couldn't say anything to a child who is merely 3 years old because she doesn't know whom she is talking about, what she is talking about, or what effect her words have on Kizie.

Due to these experiences, Kizie now avoids anything that might cause her to think about her late father. Kizie was old enough to have a rational understanding of the situation and accept the truth, but despite this, she refused to do so.

Flashback ends

Because she still isn't emotionally prepared to witness a father and daughter bonding, Kizie avoided meeting rashi's husband and didn't want to go to the airport. Kizie tried to get out of going to the airport by telling her mother that she didn't want to, but her mother wasn't about to listen to her. Rashi suspected Kizie's reluctance to go to the airport and confronted her about it, but Kizie still went, staying in a remote area where she wouldn't be seen. Knowing what was going on, Rashi called her husband and explained the situation to him, and he eventually came to meet Kizie and give her a hug, which seemed to calm her down. Do not know what to do, how to decide, or have any idea what to do. Kizie felt a great deal of affection from this hug, which was clearly not like any other she had received before. Rashi and her family came to India to check on her father's health, but instead of spending time with her father, Kaira, and Kizie, they stayed with Rashi's in-laws. This irritated Kizie, and she spent most of the rest of the trip complaining about Rashi's insistence on spending most of her time with her in-laws.

And just like that, Rashi's vacation was over, and it was time for her to return to the foreign country in which she was living, along with everyone else's, as the busyness of everyday life resumed. In particular, Kizie's grandfather, who has recently begun going out and experiencing new things and taking greater pleasure in living. And the primary goal of rashi's journey was accomplished; he was able to help Kizie's grandfather rediscover a zest for life and a sense of purpose, and to help him see how indispensable he is to his family and his community.

Kizie's grandfather enjoyed being in a place with lots of trees and plants, so it was decided to relocate there so that he would be more at ease and have more energy. Only Kizie, Kaira, Kizie's grandfather, and Rashi's family were aware that they had relocated to Rashi's house. And nobody knew about any of this.

After moving to a new location, Kizie's grandfather became more social and began to take pleasure in his new surroundings because they better reflected his personal tastes. The community was well-equipped and had all the conveniences that Kaira and Kizie needed, but they had some trouble getting to and from work and school because of the community's location on the outskirts of the city. As a result, they were able to find some inner calm. Even though it wasn't technically their residence, they were made to feel at home. They decorated the whole house as per their likings, From curtains to sofas to paintings, everything was decided by them, making the house look like a hotel. Visitors always commented on how far away it was because of its location on the outskirts of town, and how the house looked more like a hotel than a home, as if Kizie and her family were actually staying in one.

But hold on a sec: if Kizie and her family had a tragically bad 10th grade, how would her 11th grade experience be? Is it good or bad? Give it some consideration.

2

Chapter Two

What do you think, then? How do you feel about that? I was wondering how Kizie was going to be treated in the future and if her future looked bright. A glimpse into Kizie's life, but only a glimpse.

Having too much on your plate can make you not want anything else to be added to it, but life rarely works the way you expect it to.

Also, Kizie's life was not what she had hoped for. The odds weren't always in Kizie's favour. Kizie had her doubts about everything that had happened to her and even about her very existence, but she never learned to give up. Her parents gave her the fortitude to face anything that came her way, and no matter how many times she contemplated giving up, she always emerged from her setbacks even stronger in front of the world. When Kizie was feeling down, all she wanted was her dad's support. Kizie realised that even though her father was not physically present, he was the only person who supported her without her knowing it and gave her the strength to fight her own battles despite his absence. Kizie loves her father very much, but teenage is an age where teenagers often disagree with their parents, which is sometimes normal, but the reasons for fights between Kizie and her father were unusual. Kizie hated her dad because......

Flashback

Kizie was in the tenth grade when she and her family moved into a new house after her grandmother's death and began adjusting to their new normal. One day, out of the blue, rashi told Kaira that Kizie's father had been having an intimate relationship with one of their cousins ever since their parents divorced, if not before. Perhaps most baffling was the fact that word of it never spread. And yet, there were those who knew about Kaira and her boyfriend, and they weren't random bystanders or strangers; rather, they were close members of Kaira's family. Nobody ever disclosed any of this to Kaira or Kizie, despite having known it all along. When Kaira finally found out, she was devastated, and she couldn't keep it a secret from Kizie. Despite the fact that Kaira was already dealing with a lot, she knew she couldn't keep this from Kizie. Kaira was home one day when Kizie got home from school, which was very unusual because she was usually at the office. When Kizie came home for lunch, Kaira told her everything that had happened, from the beginning, to the present day, including what her father had done and the nature of his relationship. Kizie was just as upset as everyone else after hearing this; she couldn't believe her mother's account of events. Kizie's father was her first hero, as it is for most girls, but she didn't have the mental capacity to judge right from wrong at the time. Kizie's thoughts had turned to the many occasions she had witnessed her father and her so-called aunt talking or her father inquiring about her aunt or her daughter, and she had lost her appetite as a result. She went to her room and cried herself to sleep. This was something that could not be kept from Kizie despite knowing it would hurt her deeply. Kizie's head hurt like hell when she woke up, and then she remembered everything that had happened the day before. She began to dislike her father, but how could a daughter ever truly hate her own? Kizie's hatred for her father was always outweighed by her love for him, no matter how much she hated him. It's possible that a father and daughter have a relationship like this. Kizie couldn't bring herself to actively hate her father, but she did begin to keep her distance from him, which contributed to their occasional arguments.

Flashback Ends

Kizie's mother was her rock, even when she and her dad clashed.

Even though Kizie did not do well in 11th grade, she was determined to do better in 12th. She knew that her performance in this year's exams would determine whether or not she would be able to pursue higher education in the United States, or whether she would instead have to settle for a place at Delhi University or a private institution. All she knew for sure was that she couldn't risk doing well on the exams because she couldn't afford to attend a private university. It had nothing to do with family drama or social obligations, but rather, money. Kizie's father came to mind as she struggled with the fees, which should not have been an issue but became one.

Flashback

Kizie was her parents' only child, and as such, she received an abundance of attention and care. Her parents were the ideal combination of loving discipline. Kizie's mother was extremely strict about her daughter studying, but her father was the complete opposite. Regardless of the situation, he always treated Kizie with excessive affection.

Whatever Kizie pointed to or named, he would have it. And if Kizie ever had a moment of doubt between two options, her dad would gladly buy her the best of both worlds. Kizie's father has always been completely supportive of her decisions regarding her future, including her choice of major and extracurricular activities. Kizie never settled for less than what she wanted in life; she studied guitar, keyboard, and dance in equal measure. Although she had a natural talent for dance, the keyboard was her true passion. Kizie's father once bought a professional keyboard for Kizie to learn on because Kizie insisted that she learn to play the instrument. While any standard keyboard would have sufficed for practise, she insisted on and received a professional model from her father. Kizie took all the classes she wanted to in school, including French, but after her father died, her life took an unexpected turn. He had left enough money for Kizie and her sister Kaira to live comfortably without worrying about bills, but things changed when Vihaan's brother took over the family business. Kizie's uncle once told her, "You won't be getting any money because you don't have a father," in response to her request for financial assistance with school costs. That's when Kizie suffered an irreparable injury. We don't understand how anyone could have the nerve to tell her that. Who was Kizie's uncle to stop her, especially since everything belonged to Kizie's father, when she never answered her dad about where she was spending money and when he never stopped her from doing anything? Kizie never gave a second thought to the size of his father's estate or bank account because he never saw a reason to worry about such things. Her sole interests were in her family and her schoolwork. She avoided wasteful spending, which was great, but Kizie's dad also encouraged her to follow her passions and succeed at whatever she tried. Things are different when you don't have a father, and Kizie realised this for the first time when her uncle told her she had to be careful with her spending. She was ignorant of many things, despite the fact that her family had repeatedly tried to make her see the light. Because sometimes your brain is just in denial mode and refuses to accept the facts. For the first time, Kizie, the spoiled only child of her household, was denied something because she no longer had her father to provide for her.

No further memories will be recalled

She knew that no one would say no to her if she wanted to attend a private university for a specific course or other reason, but she also had a sneaking suspicion that her mother would struggle to keep up with the financial demands of her education. For this reason, she prefered to study abroad or gain admission to Delhi University instead. Kaira knew that studying abroad would be extremely expensive, but she did not care. When asked about her priorities, all she thought about was Kizie's future. Kaira simply wanted to provide the best opportunities for Kizie so that no one would ever say that Kizie's lack of success or access to the best educational opportunities was due to her father's absence. However, the primary motivation for Kaira's desire to send Kizie abroad was so that she could give her daughter a better future, free from the influence of her evil relatives and the negativity of the local population.

While juggling a million different ideas in her head, she decided to start her senior year of high school, because she knew this was her last chance to make a good impression and unlock the door to her future.

3

Chapter Three

Are you a believer in predetermined outcomes? Do you have free will in choosing your fate, or does God decide your fate for you? Or does each person create their own fate?

There is no way that things can go the way you want them to. That whole "you can't write your own destiny" nonsense isn't exactly true, is it?

At the time, Kizie's life appeared to be perfect. Kizie was doing her best to do well in school, learn what she needed to learn, and become more invested in her studies; on the other hand, Kaira was working, and Kizie's grandfather was beginning to emerge from his depression.

Kaira decided that Kizie would stay with her grandfather so that he wouldn't feel lonely and could see someone by his side and he would realise that there are people who love him, who want him because no matter what, Kizie and Kaira could not afford to lose anyone else in their family, Kizie's granny. She didn't argue with the idea because she knew how hard it was for her mum to juggle work, Kizie, and her dad, and the love she had for her grandparents. Everything was beginning to fall into place, and they were all learning to cope with life's challenges;

Kizie, in particular, was beginning to master her feelings, her schoolwork, her household duties, and her relationships with others. Kizie's social circle shrank to a select few due to her personal issues at home. Nonetheless, you can't explain your predicament to everyone or give them this reason because they don't care or aren't interested in your life. For that matter, in reality, nobody cares about anyone else's business. Kizie's family issues impacted not only her social life, but also her academic performance. She hoped that if she studied hard and got good grades, she could study abroad and improve her life.

In spite of her busy schedule and the fact that, in her mind, she didn't need or want many friends, she found contentment with her small group of close companions. One reason she didn't hang out with her friends was that she felt she needed to focus on schoolwork after a series of unfortunate events at home. However, the truth is that Kizie was once so popular that she was recognised by students as early as juniper year. At one time, she was known by everyone in the school for being the perpetually upbeat and gregarious centre of attention. Kizie didn't begin to realise the extent to which her once-extensive group of friends had shrunk until her senior year of high school, when she began to take her newfound independence more seriously. She picked up her former vigour, made an effort to find joy, became friendlier, and received overwhelming encouragement from those around her. Her close friends always knew what she was thinking, sometimes before she did.

Kizie was doing her best to maintain equilibrium, and she was also making some progress. Everything from her grades to her social life to her ability to control her own thoughts about her family to her ability to run a household efficiently was getting better. Everything was running smoothly until one day when Kaira decided to use Vihaan's office and other assets under her control to pay the bills. It wasn't as if Kaira couldn't work or didn't have the potential to do so. To make matters worse, she was juggling the needs of three households at once. Her sole motivation for taking control was to guarantee Kizie a bright future by funding her education. That is a perfectly valid interpretation. Maybe not though There is no shame in planning ahead for your child's future, especially with your own money. Every parent worries about providing a trouble-free future for their kids. Even though Vihaan worked hard to provide for Kaira's daughter, Kaira still didn't want her to go without.

Everyone's lives were altered by this one action.

What kind of impact did this have on everones' life?

4

Chapter Four

The market's reputation for Vihaan was stellar. His widespread fame as a result of his work ensured that everyone would recognise him. With Kizie's grandfather's help, he started a business from scratch, and with time and Vihaan's hard work, he grew it into an empire. From growing his company to amassing assets like homes and vehicles. He had amassed a fortune for the sole purpose of providing for Kizie's comfort and happiness in the future.

Flashback

Being the most spoiled kid in the family meant that Kizie would frequently act like a brat in the company of her loved ones. She was the spoiled one who could have anything she wanted, but she never took it for granted. Kizie was aware of her own limitations. She could be demanding, but she knew when something wasn't worth bawling over. Kizie knew where she had to act mature, no matter how immature she was in front of her loved ones. Kizie never received any negative feedback from her instructors regarding her misbehaviour or petty behaviour. Kizie has always been criticised for acting much older than she is. Kizie never understood why her teachers made these remarks; to her, it was perfectly normal behaviour. For her, these were just common courtesy rules. This was how she felt up until Kaira and Vihaan split up. Since Kizie was too young to fully comprehend the situation, she had to forego many of her wishes at the time. There were monetary, intellectual, and emotional aspects of her life that she needed to comprehend. Even though Vihaan spent most of his time at Kaira's, Kizie still had to accept the fact that she wouldn't be able to see her dad every night, that she couldn't wait up for him to get home so she could give him a big hug, and that her dad wouldn't come home and read her stories other than made-up fairy tales. Because of her parent's separation, Kizie had to become self-sufficient in many ways. There were many shifts in circumstances, but the universal affection for Kizie remained constant. The love that Vihaan and Kaira had for Kizie remained unwavering. No one could even conceive of Kizie getting a scratch. The lessons she learned from her parents' separation included taking ownership of her own actions and developing the confidence to combat the bullying she had endured.

Kizie's second period of maturity occurred after the deaths of her grandmother and Vihaan. She needed some space and time to process all that had happened and the ways in which her life had altered. When Kizie was upset one day, her mother's lap was the one place she could go to feel safe and secure, and that's why Kizie decided to rest her head there. Though she knew it would be difficult for Kizie to forget her parents so quickly, especially after witnessing their deaths in front of her eyes, she was still heartbroken to see Kizie so broken months after the incident. Kaira told Kizie that despite this, she could no longer behave in such a manner. She has her whole life ahead of her, so she shouldn't hide from her feelings or hide in a cocoon. Kaira feared that Kizie would be a naive child who would always try to avoid trouble. She knew Kizie would normally be unafraid to defend herself, but after everything that had happened, Kizie just wasn't acting like herself. And Kaira had to be tough on Kizie to get her back to where she was before, so that she can defend herself when necessary.

To everyone's knowledge, that was the last time Kizie publicly wept. Kizie made it a point to resolve that she would no longer isolate herself or cry in public. She made the conscious decision to revert to her old self, the one who is confident and can answer back to those who tease her and doesn't give a damn about what other people think. The judgments and opinions of others have never mattered to Kizie. As a matter of fact, she intended to spend the rest of her days acting on her gut instincts. She didn't want to hold herself back from accomplishing her goals and making her parents proud. She aimed to be just like her strong, independent father. Kizie aspired to be tough and brave like her dad, but her sensitive side often got in the way. Because she had a history of easily developing crushes. Even though it didn't always help, Kizie never stopped being fiercely independent and always went after what she wanted in life.

Flashback ends

Since taking over Vihaan's finances, Kaira has rented out the properties he owned so that Kizie can cover her living costs. Despite Kaira's best intentions, Vihaan's family refused to give anything to Kizie or Kaira because they believed the two were responsible for their loved one's death. But in reality, Vihaan's brother wanted everything because he didn't want to work hard and get everything his brother owned because it was enough for his family to survive until the children are old enough to earn.

The family of the late Vihaan believes that Kaira and Kizie are to blame for his death. There's no good reason for Kaira and Kizie, and especially Kizie, to wish for Vihaan's death and subsequent abandonment of them. Who would want to grow up without their dad's affection?

Instead of worrying about Vihaan, his family was more concerned with the wealth he left behind.

When Kaira took over the business and made the decision to start renting out the properties, she discovered paperwork indicating that Vihaan's brother had already changed the company's name to his own following his brother's untimely death. When someone close to you dies, it's common for your mind to wander and your emotions to cloud your judgement, but Vihaan's brother didn't let that stop him from transferring the offices to his name.

Kaira was unable to remain calm after learning this news; after all, it was Vihaan's hard work, not his brother's. However, she was also unable to formulate a plan for moving forwards, so she decided to rent out the homes immediately. Vihaan's brother did not take this well and ultimately decided to destroy Kizie's life as a result.

In this ongoing story, Vihaan's brother plotted a woman whom he falsely identified as Vihaan's second wife. But without solid evidence, you can't win your case, right? The icing on the cake is when you have strong connections, at which point it doesn't matter how right a person is or how much evidence they have to back up their claims of truth.

When the apartment was rented out, things quickly deteriorated. The woman, who was plotting with Vihaan's brother, did things that didn't make sense practically or logically, like accusing Kizie of trespassing on her father's property and filing a report of burglary. Logic would dictate that a daughter would not trespass on her father's property because she has the keys and can enter the home whenever she likes with no need to provide an explanation to anyone. She has no right to make such a demand. If not for this, it's hard to imagine a daughter stealing from either her father's or her own home. She filed a frivolous lawsuit with no supporting documentation. All the adults in the room prefered that false report to the word of one of the children. Kizie had just turned 17 years old. The information was overwhelming for her. She had no prior exposure to visiting a police station or dealing with similar situations. All she could think was that if only her father was there, none of this would have happened. No one would dare accuse Kizie or Kaira of anything, but ONLY IF. Yet now it seems as though nothing can go right. Unfortunately, Kizie and Kaira had to go through this. Kizie, who was in the 12th grade at the time, had a lot on her plate between her schoolwork, her feelings, and her family, and this complaint drama, yet she felt helpless.

This was all in the month of September, when Kizie was a senior and should have been focusing on her upcoming pre boards and doing well on them. Instead, she was worried about the events at home because she felt helpless to stop them and, more importantly, because she desperately wanted them to stop. Kizie and Kaira, who were not at fault, were implicated in this situation, either directly or indirectly. Kizie's focus on studying for her pre-boards has suffered as she and her family devote so much time and energy to finding solutions to all these problems. Kizie managed to get through the year without realising it was over, despite all the pressure she was under to do well on her final exams. Everybody was so preoccupied with their various activities that they failed to notice how quickly time had passed. Kizie and Kaira's year of managing finances was a roller coaster. Kizie felt like she had to stay inside and avoid her friends and social media because of the amount of work she had to do to keep them safe. Even if she did sneak out, Kaira would have to drop her off and pick her up, and Kizie would have to lug around her phone the whole time. Kizie was about to turn 18 and begin her board exams. Kizie was prepared mentally to give it her all on the test and get good grades, but no one can deny that she has a childlike spirit at heart, which is why she was so looking forwards to her birthday and made sure to have everything ready in advance. Unfortunately though! Once again, nothing in Kizie and Kaira's lives goes as expected. What, then, would make this work?

Their lives were so chaotic that they never knew whether they should be happy or sad; if something good happened one day, the next one would be terrible. But if there's one thing Kaira and Kizie took away from the ordeal, it was to keep going no matter how bad things seemed to be going. If you're always down in the dumps, you won't be able to appreciate the good things that happen in your life.

Kizie recognised this as the single most important piece of advice she had ever received and resolved to live her life accordingly. The lesson I took away from it was that I shouldn't put off experiencing small moments of joy because I have no idea what the future holds. If you want to stop moaning about your problems and start appreciating the little things in life, you need to stop complaining about the big ones. Kizie has always lived up to her name as someone who finds joy in the little things in life and makes others happy as a result.

Flashback

After much convincing from her father, Kaira decided to buy a new car a few months before the complaint fiasco began because she had not used her old car in quite some time. Due to the fact that everyone had different needs in a vehicle, the first place they looked was the car lots. Kizie and her grandfather, in contrast to Kaira, were interested in a car's interior and exterior quality for comfort. Then, after a great deal of research and nearly trying every car manufacturer, I decided to take the plunge. The car that Kaira's father chose was generally approved by the family, which was good news. However, Kaira was shocked to learn that her father had given the signed amount to the company and finalised the car without consulting or informing her. After completing all of his tasks, he returned home and casually informed Kaira and the others that he had arranged for a car to pick them up. For a moment, everyone was taken aback, but then again, why the hell not. After that, however, everyone agreed with the verdict. Because Kaira's dad's birthday was coming up, Kizie decided to surprise him with the car on that day. That made Kizie's grandpa very happy. On the day that Kaira was scheduled to pick up the car, her dad made a special trip to the dealership to inspect every last detail, from the seat covers to the air freshener, to ensure that everything was just as it should be. Kizie begged him to leave the office and finish the work later, but he was unmoved. He spent the entire day there ensuring that everything ran smoothly. Although Kaira would be the primary user of the vehicle, seeing the joy and pride on her father's face as he handed the keys over to her was priceless. Getting a car for his birthday made him very happy, and Kizie wanted to make sure that his special day was truly memorable, so she also made a reservation for the two of them at the hotel's most prestigious restaurant. One of his favourite hotels, and one whose atmosphere he has always appreciated, this was the primary source of his joy.

Kizie's little grandfather had left her with the taste for quality. Kizie is just like her grandfather in that she won't settle for less than the best when it comes to the hotel's ambience or the quality of an item she purchases. She would either abandon the purchase or spend more than she had planned if the item she was considering didn't spark her interest. She thought it was strange, but she ended up just like her grandfather on the subject.

Kizie ensured that her grandfather had a fantastically out-of-body experience. But what she and everyone else attending the party didn't know was that it was his last birthday.

Flashback ends

This is a lesson Kizie will never forget.

Don't chase after your good fortune because the faster you go, the farther it will run away from you. Instead, take the time to enjoy every moment because you can never predict what the future holds.

5

Chapter Five

Kizie's 18th birthday fell in the middle of her boards practical, but that didn't stop her from being excited about it or from making some plans that unfortunately did not work out.

Surely everyone has a prefered time of year. When visiting a hill station, the crisp air in the winter can be very appealing. Since the area where Kizie, Kaira, and Kizie's grandfather stayed was still being developed and was not yet fully developed, it was surrounded by greenery and shared the same cold breeze as a true hill station.

Kizie and the rest of the settlers came here because of the beautiful scenery. Kizie's grandpa needed a change of scenery to help him recover from his depression, and this place was ideal because he appreciated the natural beauty all around him. It's not wrong to appreciate nature, but it becomes wrong when you know that engaging in the activity could be harmful to you. The elderly man was Kizie's grandfather, and his body was very frail. Nobody should have to gamble with someone's health the way he had. Kaira and Kizie needed to take extreme caution with his health because the slightest miscalculation could have disastrous consequences. However, Kizie's grandfather didn't give any thought to any of this or his health. He has a weak immune system due to his numerous illnesses, but he still did not take necessary precautions. As a result, he began engaging in behaviours that were ultimately counterproductive, such as sneaking sweets, keeping the windows open during the winter even though the cold air would be bad for him, and avoiding or skipping his medication intake despite being fully aware of the potential dangers that could arise in such a scenario.

If you don't take care of yourself, it's inevitable that you'll get sick because your body can't handle the constant assault. That also happened to Kizie's grandfather. He became ill and required extended bed rest. Kizie and Kaira initially suspected the weather shift was to blame for his illness. As a result, they medicated him in the hopes that he would get better; however, when he failed to regain his strength and began to deteriorate further, Kaira realised that something was seriously wrong and that her father wouldn't get better by staying in bed. Kizie's board practicals were taking place, and Kaira had to take care of her, including transporting her to school and tuitions, because it was still not safe for Kizie to travel independently, and because there had been attempts made on her life.

Kaira couldn't choose between her grandpa and her grandfather, and she couldn't choose to abandon Kizie. Kaira, on the other hand, was aware that she must muster all her strength to convince her sisters to come over and assist her in transporting their father to the daughter for treatment. It wasn't the wrong call; being firm in certain beliefs is necessary at times. One person can't possibly handle every single thing that needs doing. Occasionally it's necessary to split the workload. The same thing was happening at Kaira's place. Since Kizie did not have anyone in her corner and there were already too many moving parts for her to keep up with, she called on her sisters for support and had them come over to help. However, it was generally understood that Kizie must do well on her SAT and ACT tests in order to gain admission to a public university; she cannot attend a private institution.

Anika and Ekta, Kaira's sisters, came to see him after much persuasion, and after looking at him, everyone had a sneaking suspicion that there isn't much time left, and that maybe if he went to the hospital this time, he wouldn't be coming back to home.

How do you feel about that? Could Anika and Ekta aid Kaira, or would they merely provide her with more excuses to do nothing?

6

Chapter Six

Anika and Ekta were asked to come and talk to their father about how his current lifestyle is harmful to his health, but they refused, citing the age-old excuse that they are too busy taking care of their own families. This statement did not sit well with Kaira and she responded bluntly, telling them that she would not be taking any responsibility and that she and her sister Kizie needed to go see their father.

Anika and Ekta, having heard all this, came to see their father despite knowing that he doesn't have much time and that there's no assurance that he'll return to normal this time. No one could have been unaware of his condition, and he himself may have realised that he was too frail to survive at this point. When his condition worsened, it was decided he needed to be admitted to the hospital, but the big question now was who would take him there and stay with him until he recovered. Everyone, as usual, directed their attention to Kaira and Kizie. As if he were only Matt's father and not their father, everyone assumed that Kaira would take care of him, but she did not. But this time, Kaira made her decision public: she told the hospital staff that she would not be staying because her daughter Kizie needed her presence at her upcoming board practicals.

While listening to the conversation, Kizie couldn't help but feel relieved that she had been her mother's top priority this time around. That didn't mean she didn't care about her grandfather or love him. Because he was all she had left, she worried about him and loved him deeply. Even though she only had her mother and grandfather to rely on for support, she wanted to be self-centered in this situation because it would have such far-reaching implications for her life and career if she didn't get what she wanted.

Alas! Nothing ever goes well with Ekta and Anika, and they immediately began harping on the fact that it is Kaira's duty to take care of her father.

To put the final nail in Kizie's coffin, Anika said, "Her grandfather is not just Kaira's father but their father, and why should we be the only one to look after him when all you come in happy times and when it is time to take gifts?" Kizie lost her temper and blurted out to Anika, "Her grandfather is not just Kaira's father but their father." You guys are always there for each other, but when it comes to taking care of your own dad, you suddenly start to value your own family. Because the same old excuse was used—that they had to take care of their husband, children, and in-laws—Kizie was so incensed that she didn't even realise what she was saying. Also, Kizie retorts, "You all are behaving with us like this because I do not have a father and my mother does not have a husband, right? Nothing like this would have happened if my dad were here today. I took a week off of school in 12th grade to stay at the hospital because none of you showed up to look after your father, and you didn't come to our house for an entire year when it was your daughter's boards. Apropos, wouldn't you say? When I really needed her help, my mum was taking care of her elderly father. I never once complained that my mum was too busy with work or the hospital or the office to spend time with me, but now that I really need her, you guys can't even help us out. After Anika told Kizie that she would never visit their house again if it bothered her, Kizie knew she had said too much, but she couldn't help herself. Kizie was hurt by what Anika said about her grandfather, as if Kizie cared about what Anika said in the first place. Neither Kizie nor Kaira ever desired it. No one else was related to either of them besides Kaira's father. Kizie was aware that she had said quite a bit, but she also knew that Anika needed to air her thoughts. Neither Kaira nor Anika said anything to Kizie about it, as they both understood the necessity of such an outburst, especially considering that Kizie's professional future hinged on the outcome of the board meeting.

Kizie never complained when Kaira took care of her parents, probably because she loved her grandparents just as much, if not more, than her own. And it has never happened that Kizie or Kaira have shied away from their responsibilities towards their parents; in fact, there have been times when they have taken Kaira's mother to the hospital in the middle of the night and spent the entire time there caring for her; upon their return the following morning, Kizie would go to school, and Kaira would go to her office. In that moment, nobody spoke up. Kizie had never been one to demand attention or respond negatively when Kaira's sister asked to come and look after their mother, but this time it all got to be too much for her and she exploded.

It was decided after this outburst that Ekta would take her father home with her and then take him to the doctor the following day.

7

Chapter Seven

Is it ever a problem when a daughter invites her parents over? You don't think there'll be any trouble, do you? Even Ekta wasn't bothered, but then rashi, who wasn't even there to help, chimed in and implied once more that it was Kaira's job to look after her dad. Neither Kizie nor Kaira reacted to this, however, and Ekta and Kaira both let her say whatever she wanted.

The following day, Ekta took her father to the clinic, where he underwent a battery of tests that revealed his condition to be extremely dire and the urgency with which he required admission. Once more, however, the question of who would remain in the hospital arose. The reason Anika gave for her firm refusal was that her husband would not approve. After that, I asked Kaira, but she said no because right now Kizie was more important to her, and I couldn't ask rashi because she wasn't even in India. Ekta was the only one left, but she, too, had to stay home and take care of her family.

In the end, Ekta would only visit her father twice a day, for one hour each time. Is it so difficult to take care of your own parents that you can't even be there for them when they're at their most vulnerable in the hospital? What's the point if you can't be there for someone when they need you or when they're at their most vulnerable? Kaira and Kizie were furious and disappointed to learn that Ekta had abandoned their sick father at the hospital, a place they would never leave him alone if they had the choice; however, they were both preoccupied with studying for upcoming board exams and had no choice but to leave him unattended. Kizie felt uneasy about her grandfather's hospital stay because he was there by himself. They tried to reason with Ekta and convince her that she should visit her sick father in the hospital, but Ekta was adamant about staying with her husband. Though your husband certainly deserves your attention, there are times when your parents must come first. Can't you spare a few days to honour those who have given so much for you? But no, Ekta did not change her mind, and neither Kaira nor Kizie could do anything about it other than feel bad about it. Both Kizie and Kaira made it a point to keep in daily contact with their dad while they were away at college.

Kizie's 18th birthday was coming up, and she'd been looking forwards to spending the day at home with her grandfather and mother, followed by going out to dinner and opening a bottle of champagne, but those plans fell through when her grandfather was admitted to the hospital and she had to prioritise studying for her board exams instead.

But you know what they say about how just when everything goes wrong, something good happens, right? In the same vein, Kizie's special day also ended up being a pleasant surprise. Kizie had no grand plans for her birthday and was content to spend the day at home with her mother when a friend came over to surprise her. This turned what could have been a dull day into a memorable one, though Kizie still missed her grandfather. Except for rashi, everyone wished her a happy birthday. Kizie waited all day for rash to call, but when she didn't, Kaira gave her a call. When rash's husband answered, he seemed perfectly normal. In fact, Kaira did try to drop hints about Kizie's birthday, but he missed them. Kizie asked her mum not to tell him it was her birthday, but Kaira went ahead and told him anyway. Due to her high regard for them, Kizie was let down by their behaviour; in fact, she unintentionally shed a few tears when they forgot her birthday. She ignored them and instead concentrated on the unexpected visitors: her friends.

People who love and care for you deserve your attention and affection.

After all was said and done, Kizie had a wonderful 18th birthday.

Even Kizie's grandfather got better after her birthday, and was scheduled for discharge. Kizie spoke to her grandfather the day before he was discharged, and he expressed his displeasure at having to spend so much time in the hospital alone with no visitors. It was a way of subtly slapping in the face those who had abandoned her father at a time of great need. Kizie informed Kaira about her grandfather's condition as soon as she learned of it, and the two of them spent the next day arranging for his release from the hospital. And, naturally, his face lit up at the sight of Kizie and Kaira, which, in turn, brought a smile to Kizie's face because she loved seeing her grandfather happy. And with that, Kaira and Kizie brought him back home. Though he was healthy, Kizie and Kaira had to be watchful with his diet and medication.

8

Chapter Eight

Kizie's board exams, about which she was very anxious and uncertain, began shortly after her grandfather returned home. She made it a point to focus solely on her schoolwork and do her best on her exams.

Even though Kizie did her best to study for her exams, she was unable to because the problems that Vihaan's brother had initially caused had not been resolved and had instead reached a crisis point. She'd sometimes have to spend days in the police station before her exams just to finish meaningless paperwork. Once again, there was a lot for Kizie to process and remember. She spent late nights studying for her boards with nothing but coffee and books.

This was the crux of the situation, Kizie's board exams. Kizie felt jittery, worried, and all that other nonsense. Given that passing or failing the board exams was of equal importance. Kaira realised Kizie was going through a tough time and would benefit from some encouragement. Kaira made extra efforts the night before Kizie's exams to reassure her and ensure that Kizie wouldn't put undue stress on herself.

Everything seemed to be running smoothly. Kizie had been studying hard and doing her best on her exams, but as her grandfather began to improve, he began leaving the house once more—without telling Kizie or Kaira, and sometimes even leaving the front door unlocked. Kizie had a dilemma: her grandfather wanted to go out and have fun, but she and her sister Kaira had to study for an exam in a subject Kizie detested. Again, the question arose as to who would look after him, given that it is not safe to leave the front door propped open and that Kizie needs to focus on her exams and cannot afford to miss them.

When Kaira asked Ekta and Anika to come over and explain this to their father, they again refused. However, they also knew that whatever happened the last time would actually affect the relations and that they too have some responsibility towards their father, so they came this time and tried to explain things to him, but he didn't understand. As a result, it was decided that Ekta would take him to her house until Kizie's board exams g were over. Even though neither Kizie nor Mamata wanted it, they understood that it was necessary at the time for Kizie. The occasional act of selfishness is acceptable.

There's nothing wrong with being selfish, and there are times when it's necessary both to get things done and to serve as an example to others.

Rashi began to point out once more that it is Kaira's responsibility to take care of their father and none of theirs when Ekta decided to take him to her house. Kaira and Kizie were annoyed, but instead of telling her so, they began avoiding her because whenever they brought up the topic, rashi would bring up how Ekta's household is more important than Kizie's boards or caring for their father. For Kizie, the only issue was whether or not rashi was genuine.

I can't believe she said that.

Even though Kaira knew that Kizie despises and is weakest in this subject, she stayed by her side as she studied for Kizie's final exam anyway.

In the year 2020, when Kizie was making her boards, the deadly COVID-19 pandemic struck, causing almost every country to go into lockdown. The country went into lockdown just three days before the exam, so the whole thing was postponed. However, Kaira's dad was staying at Ekta's house, which was wrong because nobody knew how long the lockdown would last. And that's why Kizie and rashi were at odds once more. But after this schism, Kaira wasted no time in making plans to bring her father home to live with her and Kizie again from ekta's place.

Kizie's board exams kept getting postponed as the number of reported cases rose and the country went into lockdown, and in some ways, she was relieved that she wouldn't have to show up to take the exam in the subject she finds the least interesting.

Although the lockdown was lifted and people began venturing out again after a couple of months, Kizie and her grandfather spent most of their time inside. Kizie suffered from a dust allergy that made it difficult for her to breathe, and her grandfather had a compromised immune system, so they didn't want to risk either of their conditions.

Kizie and her grandfather spent the entire month of June 2020 at home, but despite their constant presence, Kizie's grandfather began to feel ill. Not from COVID-19, but rather his chronic illnesses, which had gotten progressively worse over time. Kaira's gut told her that her father didn't have long to live, and the signs pointed to the fact that something very serious had happened to him and that he was in a critical condition. Even Kizie had an inkling that he was merely extending his life, and she kept this to herself. Kaira consulted their family doctor online because there weren't many doctors available for in-person consultations due to the spread of COVID-19, and he was in a critical and deteriorating condition. While the doctor did write a few prescriptions, he also told Kaira that her father doesn't have long to live, and that she and her sister Kizie should get ready for that.

Since their husbands and in-laws are more important than their own father, Kaira shared all of this information with her sister, who eventually paid a visit to their father two days later. Rashi was unable to join her friends Anika and Ekta on their visit because she was stuck in Australia due to the COVID-19 travel ban. As a result, Ekta and Anika's father's terminal condition was immediately apparent to them upon their first sighting. Additionally, there are times when people truly believe that this is their lucky day. Perhaps he, too, was one of the lucky few who occasionally experiences such intuitive insights. He didn't say so to Kaira or anyone else, but he was aware of the truth and, perhaps because his illness had made him so frail, had prepared himself for it. Despite his best efforts, he was ultimately unsuccessful in his attempt to reclaim his life. Kizie made it a point to celebrate even the smallest of events with her ailing father because she never knew when their time together would be up.

Kizie, as she did every year, visited her grandfather on Father's Day to give him her heartfelt greetings. This year, however, her wish brought him more joy than he could have imagined, and he beamed with a smile so bright that it brought tears to his eyes. Kizie was smiling and wishing her grandfather a happy father's day, but only she knew how hard she was fighting back the tears she was holding back so she wouldn't appear weak in front of him. Perhaps the fulfilment of that one wish brightened his entire day. In order to cheer him up, Kizie had a bouquet and cake delivered. When his coworkers or servants questioned his perpetual good mood, he would simply reply, "Today is my day, and that is why I am so happy."

A short time after Father's Day, it was his birthday, and Kizie planned a party for him. For once she wanted to deny the possibility that this birthday would be her last spent with her grandfather. She knew this to be true because the doctors had told her so, but she wished she could make a different reality instead. However, she could only hope.

He was admitted to the hospital three days before he passed away. Again, when Kaira and Kizie called Anika and ekta to let them know what was going on, they were told they couldn't come because their priorities weren't the same as theirs. On the same day, at night, Kaira became ill and in excruciating pain. Kizie invited ekta and Anika over, but they had to decline once again due to other commitments. Kizie was so aggravated that she told them bluntly that they need not come to her house at any time, as she would take care of everyone and would even go and meet the doctor alone if necessary, and that Kaira was too weak to go to the hospital tomorrow to see the doctor, and that they were more worried about the husband than their father. The news that Kizie's grandfather had suffered a heart attack from the doctor the following day came as a shock to everyone. In spite of what anyone says, Kaira felt obligated to keep her sisters apprised of her father's condition. After hearing the diagnosis of a heart attack, it was obvious to Kaira and Kizie, and the doctors confirmed their suspicions, that he didn't have long to live. Kaira still tried to contact their family doctor in an effort to save her father's life, but he advised against it, saying that if his heart were treated, his kidneys would fail and vice versa, and that in either case, he would need to be placed on a ventilator. Hearing this, Kaira made the difficult decision to let her father suffer until he passed away without treatment.

In the end, Ekta and Anika did not visit their dad. Kaira made it abundantly clear to her siblings that her father had suffered a heart attack and did not have long to live, but they still did not act until after rashi. Anika and ekta came to see their dad because their mum called them and reassured them he was okay. Anika, Kizie, and Kaira met him in the hospital the day after they arrived. Kizie was the first to approach the door, and she introduced herself. Seeing his condition made her want to cry, but she knew she needed to put on a brave face for her daughter. The two of them met, and he smiled at her and held her hands as if to show his love and affection. Perhaps due to his frailty or the side effects of his medications, he did not recognise anyone. Kaira was the last person to see him alive, and as soon as he did, he closed his eyes in front of her and left, leaving everyone broken behind. Everyone was relieved that he no longer had to suffer and that he could finally be with his wife, but Kaira and Kizie felt the impact the most because they were the ones who were with him until the end. Nobody can put themselves in their shoes or understand how they must be feeling.

9

Chapter Nine

"Life is full of surprises."

Given that this is their current reality, Kizie and Kaira knew nothing else. Kaira and Kizie were each other's only support system now.

After the news of the tragedy spread, it was decided that students would not have to take their final exams but would instead be graded on their overall performance in the classroom. Here's another thing that's causing Kizie anxiety. Both Kizie and Kaira were incredibly anxious about Kizie's performance on her upcoming board exams.

The day had come, the day that would determine Kizie's fate, the day that would reveal whether or not she had been successful in proving herself and whether or not her efforts had paid off. Kizie's anxiety level was through the roof. Given that it was a government website and so many students were trying to log in as soon as the results were announced, the website where students could see their percentage crashed. Even Kizie was unable to access the website, but she was so eager to learn her score that she called everyone she could think of and gave them the information they needed to view it for themselves. Sadly, the website was inaccessible.

Soon, one of Kizie's cousins would have access to the findings. During the time that Kizie's cousin was verifying the findings, they were both available. She began keeping track of her grades, and when she saw that she had gotten a mark that was literally beyond her wildest dreams (95%), she let out an uncontrollable scream of joy. Kizie and Kaira felt like they were in a dream, but deep down they desperately missed their parents.

Family members called as usual to find out how Kizie did, despite their certainty that she didn't do better than a 70%. Kizie and Kaira both found it hard to believe her 95% score on her board exams, but it was the truth.

It took some time for the news to sink in, and some people were jealous of Kizie because they had lower scores. Even Kizie's own family members told Kaira that they were surprised by Kizie's high score because they hadn't expected it. People have speculated that you may have bribed members of the board, and there was even a rumour that Kizie had lied about performing poorly on two of her exams.

It's true that "life is full of surprises."

That's why it is said

"When you least expect it, the unexpected happens. Because of this, you should never give up hope and should always do your best."

Now was the time for a new chapter to unlock in Khushi's and Mamta's life. How would this new chapter would be? Exciting, struggling, or emotional?

Would everyone's relation be same or get changed?

Would khushi and mamta be same?

How would be Khushi's new journey to her college be like?

So many questions right?

Before answering these questions here is something for you to think about.

How does it actually feel getting away from family and your parents, especially for a girl? Getting married and then going to a different home or a state or a different country has always been tough and those emotions are always different and no one can experience that or explain that. That can only be felt by the girl, her parents, and the closest family members. No matter how much your husband loves you. He too can't even experience that. But has anyone ever thought about this from the girl's point of view? Those emotions and feelings can neither be written in words nor explained them in words.

Wait till the next part of the series to get all your answers.

"People change and so do relations and their equations change."

9 798889 091400

Printed by Libri Plureos GmbH in Hamburg,
Germany